MORE
TALES FROM
BEATRIX POTTER

MORE
TALES FROM
BEATRIX POTTER

THE ORIGINAL AND AUTHORIZED EDITIONS
BY BEATRIX POTTER

™

WHSMITH

EXCLUSIVE
· BOOKS ·

FREDERICK WARNE
Penguin Books Ltd, Harmondsworth, Middlesex, England
Viking Penguin Inc., 40 West 23rd Street, New York, New York 10010, U.S.A.
Penguin Books Australia Ltd, Ringwood, Victoria, Australia
Penguin Books Canada Limited, 2801 John Street, Markham, Ontario, Canada L3R 1B4
Penguin Books (N.Z.) Ltd, 182–190 Wairau Road, Auckland 10, New Zealand

First published in this edition 1985
Reprinted 1986
This edition copyright © Frederick Warne & Co., 1985

ISBN 0 7232 3359 4

Printed and bound in Great Britain by
William Clowes Limited, Beccles and London

Contents

THE TALE OF
SQUIRREL NUTKIN

THIS is a Tale about a tail—a tail
that belonged to a little red squirrel,
and his name was Nutkin.

He had a brother called Twinkleberry, and a great many cousins: they
lived in a wood at the edge of a lake.

IN the middle of the lake there is an
island covered with trees and nut
bushes; and amongst those trees stands
a hollow oak-tree, which is the house
of an owl who is called Old Brown.

ONE autumn when the nuts were ripe, and the leaves on the hazel bushes were golden and green—Nutkin and Twinkleberry and all the other little squirrels came out of the wood, and down to the edge of the lake.

THEY made little rafts out of twigs,
and they paddled away over the
water to Owl Island to gather nuts.

Each squirrel had a little sack and a
large oar, and spread out his tail for a
sail.

THEY also took with them an offer-
ing of three fat mice as a present
for Old Brown, and put them down
upon his door-step.

Then Twinkleberry and the other
little squirrels each made a low bow,
and said politely—

'Old Mr. Brown, will you favour us
with permission to gather nuts upon
your island?'

BUT Nutkin was excessively impertinent in his manners. He bobbed
up and down like a little red *cherry*,
singing—

'Riddle me, riddle me, rot-tot-tote!
A little wee man, in a red red coat!
A staff in his hand, and a stone in his throat;
If you'll tell me this riddle, I'll give you a groat.'

Now this riddle is as old as the hills;
Mr. Brown paid no attention whatever
to Nutkin.

He shut his eyes obstinately and
went to sleep.

THE squirrels filled their little sacks
with nuts, and sailed away home
in the evening.

BUT next morning they all came back again to Owl Island; and Twinkleberry and the others brought a fine fat mole, and laid it on the stone in front of Old Brown's doorway, and said—

'Mr. Brown, will you favour us with your gracious permission to gather some more nuts?'

BUT Nutkin, who had no respect, began to dance up and down, tickling old Mr. Brown with a *nettle* and singing—

'Old Mr. B! Riddle-me-ree!
Hitty Pitty within the wall,
Hitty Pitty without the wall;
If you touch Hitty Pitty,
Hitty Pitty will bite you!'

Mr. Brown woke up suddenly and carried the mole into his house.

HE shut the door in Nutkin's face.
Presently a little thread of blue
smoke from a wood fire came up from
the top of the tree, and Nutkin peeped
through the key-hole and sang—

'A house full, a hole full!
And you cannot gather a bowl-full!'

THE squirrels searched for nuts all over the island and filled their little sacks.

But Nutkin gathered oak-apples— yellow and scarlet—and sat upon a beech-stump playing marbles, and watching the door of old Mr. Brown.

ON the third day the squirrels got up very early and went fishing; they caught seven fat minnows as a present for Old Brown.

They paddled over the lake and landed under a crooked chestnut tree on Owl Island.

TWINKLEBERRY and six other little squirrels each carried a fat minnow; but Nutkin, who had no nice manners, brought no present at all. He ran in front, singing—

'The man in the wilderness said to me,
"How many strawberries grow in the sea?"
I answered him as I thought good—
"As many red herrings as grow in the wood."'

But old Mr. Brown took no interest in riddles—not even when the answer was provided for him.

ON the fourth day the squirrels brought a present of six fat beetles, which were as good as plums in *plum-pudding* for Old Brown. Each beetle was wrapped up carefully in a dock-leaf, fastened with a pine-needle pin.

But Nutkin sang as rudely as ever—

'Old Mr. B! riddle-me-ree
  Flour of England, fruit of Spain,
  Met together in a shower of rain;
  Put in a bag tied round with a string,
If you'll tell me this riddle, I'll give you a ring!'

Which was ridiculous of Nutkin, because he had not got any ring to give to Old Brown.

THE other squirrels hunted up and down the nut bushes; but Nutkin gathered robin's pin-cushions off a briar bush, and stuck them full of pine-needle pins.

ON the fifth day the squirrels
brought a present of wild honey;
it was so sweet and sticky that they
licked their fingers as they put it down
upon the stone. They had stolen it out
of a bumble *bees'* nest on the tippitty
top of the hill.

But Nutkin skipped up and down,
singing—

'Hum-a-bum! buzz! buzz! Hum-a-bum buzz!
    As I went over Tipple-tine
    I met a flock of bonny swine;
Some yellow-nacked, some yellow backed!
    They were the very bonniest swine
    That e'er went over Tipple-tine.'

OLD Mr. Brown turned up his eyes
in disgust at the impertinence of
Nutkin.

But he ate up the honey!

THE squirrels filled their little sacks
with nuts.

But Nutkin sat upon a big flat rock,
and played ninepins with a crab apple
and green fir-cones.

ON the sixth day, which was Saturday, the squirrels came again for
the last time; they brought a new-laid
egg in a little rush basket as a last
parting present for Old Brown.

But Nutkin ran in front laughing,
and shouting—

> 'Humpty Dumpty lies in the beck,
> With a white counterpane round his neck,
> Forty doctors and forty wrights,
> Cannot put Humpty Dumpty to rights!'

NOW old Mr. Brown took an interest in eggs; he opened one eye
and shut it again. But still he did not
speak.

NUTKIN became more and more impertinent—

'Old Mr. B! Old Mr. B!
Hickamore, Hackamore, on the King's kitchen door;
All the King's horses, and all the King's men,
Couldn't drive Hickamore, Hackamore,
Off the King's kitchen door.'

Nutkin danced up and down like a *sunbeam*; but still Old Brown said nothing at all.

Nutkin began again—

'Arthur O'Bower has broken his band,
He comes roaring up the land!
The King of Scots with all his power,
Cannot turn Arthur of the Bower!'

NUTKIN made a whirring noise to sound like the *wind*, and he took a running jump right onto the head of Old Brown!....

Then all at once there was a flutterment and a scufflement and a loud 'Squeak!'

The other squirrels scuttered away into the bushes.

WHEN they came back very cautiously, peeping round the tree— there was Old Brown sitting on his door-step, quite still, with his eyes closed, as if nothing had happened.

*   *   *   *   *

But Nutkin was in his waist-coat pocket!

THIS looks like the end of the story; but it isn't.

OLD BROWN carried Nutkin into his house, and held him up by the tail, intending to skin him; but Nutkin pulled so very hard that his tail broke in two, and he dashed up the staircase and escaped out of the attic window.

AND to this day, if you meet Nutkin up a tree and ask him a riddle, he will throw sticks at you, and stamp his feet and scold, and shout—

'Cuck-cuck-cuck-cur-r-r-cuck-k-k!'

THE STORY OF
A FIERCE BAD RABBIT

THIS is a fierce bad Rabbit; look
at his savage whiskers, and his
claws and his turned-up tail.

THIS is a nice gentle Rabbit. His
mother has given him a carrot.

THE bad Rabbit would like some carrot.

H E doesn't say 'Please.' He takes it!

AND he scratches the good Rabbit
very badly.

THE good Rabbit creeps away, and
hides in a hole. It feels sad.

THIS is a man with a gun.

HE sees something sitting on a bench. He thinks it is a very funny bird!

HE comes creeping up behind the trees.

A<small>ND</small> then he shoots—B<small>ANG</small>!

THIS is what happens—

BUT this is all he finds on the bench, when he rushes up with his gun.

THE good Rabbit peeps out of its hole,

AND it sees the bad Rabbit tearing past—without any tail or whiskers!

THE STORY OF MISS MOPPET

THIS is a Pussy called Miss Moppet,
she thinks she has heard a mouse!

THIS is the Mouse peeping out behind the cupboard, and making fun of Miss Moppet. He is not afraid of a kitten.

THIS is Miss Moppet jumping just too late; she misses the Mouse and hits her own head.

S HE thinks it is a very hard cup-board!

THE Mouse watches Miss Moppet
from the top of the cupboard.

MISS MOPPET ties up her head
in a duster, and sits before the
fire.

THE Mouse thinks she is looking very ill. He comes sliding down the bell-pull.

M ISS MOPPET looks worse and
worse. The Mouse comes a little
nearer.

MISS MOPPET holds her poor
head in her paws, and looks at
him through a hole in the duster. The
Mouse comes *very* close.

AND then all of a sudden—Miss
Moppet jumps upon the Mouse!

AND because the Mouse has teased
Miss Moppet—Miss Moppet thinks
she will tease the Mouse; which is not
at all nice of Miss Moppet.

SHE ties him up in the duster, and tosses it about like a ball.

B UT she forgot about that hole in
the duster; and when she untied
it—there was no Mouse!

HE has wriggled out and run away; and he is dancing a jig on the top of the cupboard!

The Tale of
Samuel Whiskers
or
The Roly-Poly Pudding

ONCE upon a time there was an old cat, called Mrs. Tabitha Twitchit, who was an anxious parent. She used to lose her kittens continually, and whenever they were lost they were always in mischief!

On baking day she determined to shut them up in a cupboard.

She caught Moppet and Mittens, but she could not find Tom.

Mrs. Tabitha went up and down all

over the house, mewing for Tom Kitten. She looked in the pantry under the staircase, and she searched the best spare bedroom that was all covered up with dust sheets. She went right upstairs and looked into the attics, but she could not find him anywhere.

It was an old, old house, full of cupboards and passages. Some of the walls were four feet thick, and there used to be queer noises inside them, as if there might be a little secret staircase. Certainly there were odd little jagged doorways in the wainscot, and things disappeared at night—especially cheese and bacon.

Mrs. Tabitha became more and more distracted, and mewed dreadfully.

While their mother was searching the house, Moppet and Mittens had got into mischief.

The cupboard door was not locked, so they pushed it open and came out.

They went straight to the dough
which was set to rise in a pan before
the fire.

They patted it with their little soft
paws–'Shall we make dear little muf-
fins?' said Mittens to Moppet.

But just at that moment somebody
knocked at the front door, and Moppet
jumped into the flour barrel in a fright.

Mittens ran away to the dairy, and hid in an empty jar on the stone shelf where the milk pans stand.

The visitor was a neighbour, Mrs. Ribby; she had called to borrow some yeast.

Mrs. Tabitha came downstairs mewing dreadfully—'Come in, Cousin Ribby, come in, and sit ye down! I'm in sad trouble, Cousin Ribby,' said Tabitha, shedding tears. 'I've lost my dear son Thomas; I'm afraid the rats have got him.' She wiped her eyes with her apron.

'He's a bad kitten, Cousin Tabitha; he made a cat's cradle of my best

bonnet last time I came to tea. Where
have you looked for him?'

'All over the house! The rats are
too many for me. What a thing it is
to have an unruly family!' said Mrs.
Tabitha Twitchit.

'I'm not afraid of rats; I will help you to find him; and whip him too! What is all that soot in the fender?'

'The chimney wants sweeping—Oh, dear me, Cousin Ribby—now Moppet and Mittens are gone!'

'They have both got out of the cupboard!'

Ribby and Tabitha set to work to search the house thoroughly again. They poked under the beds with Ribby's umbrella, and they rummaged in cupboards. They even fetched a candle, and looked inside a clothes chest in one of the attics. They could not find

anything, but once they heard a door bang and somebody scuttered down-stairs.

'Yes, it is infested with rats,' said Tabitha tearfully. 'I caught seven young ones out of one hole in the back kitchen, and we had them for dinner last Saturday. And once I saw the old father rat—an enormous old rat, Cousin Ribby. I was just going to jump upon him, when he showed his yellow teeth at me and whisked down the hole.'

'The rats get upon my nerves, Cousin Ribby,' said Tabitha.

Ribby and Tabitha searched and searched. They both heard a curious roly-poly noise under the attic floor. But there was nothing to be seen.

They returned to the kitchen. 'Here's one of your kittens at least,' said Ribby, dragging Moppet out of the flour barrel.

They shook the flour off her and set her down on the kitchen floor. She seemed to be in a terrible fright.

'Oh! Mother, Mother,' said Moppet, 'there's been an old woman rat in the kitchen, and she's stolen some of the dough!'

The two cats ran to look at the dough pan. Sure enough there were marks of little scratching fingers, and a lump of dough was gone!

'Which way did she go, Moppet?'

But Moppet had been too much frightened to peep out of the barrel again.

Ribby and Tabitha took her with them to keep her safely in sight, while they went on with their search.

They went into the dairy.

The first thing they found was Mittens, hiding in an empty jar.

They tipped up the jar, and she scrambled out.

'Oh, Mother, Mother!' said Mittens—

'Oh! Mother, Mother, there has been an old man rat in the dairy—a dreadful 'normous big rat, mother; and he's stolen a pat of butter and the rolling-pin.'

Ribby and Tabitha looked at one another.

'A rolling-pin and butter! Oh, my poor son Thomas!' exclaimed Tabitha, wringing her paws.

'A rolling-pin?' said Ribby. 'Did we not hear a roly-poly noise in the attic when we were looking into that chest?'

Ribby and Tabitha rushed upstairs again. Sure enough the roly-poly noise was still going on quite distinctly under the attic floor.

'This is serious, Cousin Tabitha,' said Ribby. 'We must send for John Joiner at once, with a saw.'

* * * * *

Now this is what had been happening to Tom Kitten, and it shows how very unwise it is to go up a chimney in a very old house, where a person does not know his way, and where there are enormous rats.

Tom Kitten did not want to be shut up in a cupboard. When he saw that his mother was going to bake, he determined to hide.

He looked about for a nice convenient place, and he fixed upon the chimney.

The fire had only just been lighted, and it was not hot; but there was a

white choky smoke from the green sticks. Tom Kitten got upon the fender and looked up. It was a big old-fashioned fire-place.

The chimney itself was wide enough inside for a man to stand up and walk about. So there was plenty of room for a little Tom Cat.

He jumped right up into the fire-place, balancing himself upon the iron bar where the kettle hangs.

Tom Kitten took another big jump

off the bar, and landed on a ledge high up inside the chimney, knocking down some soot into the fender.

Tom Kitten coughed and choked with the smoke; and he could hear the sticks beginning to crackle and burn in the fire-place down below. He made up his mind to climb right to the top, and get out on the slates, and try to catch sparrows.

'I cannot go back. If I slipped I might fall in the fire and singe my beautiful tail and my little blue jacket.'

The chimney was a very big old-fashioned one. It was built in the days when people burnt logs of wood upon the hearth.

The chimney stack stood up above the roof like a little stone tower, and the daylight shone down from the top, under the slanting slates that kept out the rain.

Tom Kitten was getting very frightened! He climbed up, and up, and up.

Then he waded sideways through inches of soot. He was like a little sweep himself.

It was most confusing in the dark.
One flue seemed to lead into another.

There was less smoke, but Tom
Kitten felt quite lost.

He scrambled up and up; but before
he reached the chimney top he came
to a place where somebody had loos-
ened a stone in the wall. There were
some mutton bones lying about—

'This seems funny,' said Tom Kitten.
'Who has been gnawing bones up here
in the chimney? I wish I had never
come! And what a funny smell? It is
something like mouse; only dreadfully
strong. It makes me sneeze,' said Tom
Kitten.

He squeezed through the hole in the wall, and dragged himself along a most uncomfortably tight passage where there was scarcely any light.

He groped his way carefully for several yards; he was at the back of the skirting-board in the attic, where there is a little mark * in the picture.

All at once he fell head over heels in the dark, down a hole, and landed on a heap of very dirty rags.

When Tom Kitten picked himself up and looked about him—he found himself in a place that he had never seen before, although he had lived all his life in the house.

It was a very small stuffy fusty room, with boards, and rafters, and cobwebs, and lath and plaster.

Opposite to him—as far away as he could sit—was an enormous rat.

'What do you mean by tumbling
into my bed all covered with smuts?'
said the rat, chattering his teeth.

'Please sir, the chimney wants sweeping,' said poor Tom Kitten.

'Anna Maria! Anna Maria!' squeaked
the rat. There was a pattering noise
and an old woman rat poked her head
round a rafter.

All in a minute she rushed upon
Tom Kitten, and before he knew what
was happening—

His coat was pulled off, and he was
rolled up in a bundle, and tied with
string in very hard knots.

Anna Maria did the tying. The old
rat watched her and took snuff. When
she had finished, they both sat staring
at him with their mouths open.

'Anna Maria,' said the old man rat (whose name was Samuel Whiskers),— 'Anna Maria, make me a kitten dumpling roly-poly pudding for my dinner.'

'It requires dough and a pat of butter, and a rolling-pin,' said Anna Maria, considering Tom Kitten with her head on one side.

'No,' said Samuel Whiskers, 'make it properly, Anna Maria, with bread-crumbs.'

'Nonsense! Butter and dough,' replied Anna Maria.

The two rats consulted together for a few minutes and then went away. Samuel Whiskers got through a

hole in the wainscot, and went boldly
down the front staircase to the dairy
to get the butter. He did not meet
anybody.

He made a second journey for the
rolling-pin. He pushed it in front of
him with his paws, like a brewer's man
trundling a barrel.

He could hear Ribby and Tabitha
talking, but they were busy lighting
the candle to look into the chest.

They did not see him.

Anna Maria went down by way of the skirting-board and a window shutter to the kitchen to steal the dough.

She borrowed a small saucer, and scooped up the dough with her paws.

She did not observe Moppet.

While Tom Kitten was left alone under the floor of the attic, he wriggled about and tried to mew for help.

But his mouth was full of soot and cobwebs, and he was tied up in such very tight knots, he could not make anybody hear him.

Except a spider, which came out of a crack in the ceiling and examined the knots critically, from a safe distance.

It was a judge of knots because it had a habit of tying up unfortunate blue-bottles. It did not offer to assist him.

Tom Kitten wriggled and squirmed until he was quite exhausted.

Presently the rats came back and set to work to make him into a dumpling. First they smeared him with butter, and then they rolled him in the dough.

'Will not the string be very indigestible, Anna Maria?' inquired Samuel Whiskers.

Anna Maria said she thought that it was of no consequence; but she wished that Tom Kitten would hold his head still, as it disarranged the pastry. She laid hold of his ears.

Tom Kitten bit and spat, and mewed and wriggled; and the rolling-pin went roly-poly, roly; roly, poly, roly. The rats each held an end.

'His tail is sticking out! You did not fetch enough dough, Anna Maria.'

'I fetched as much as I could carry,' replied Anna Maria.

'I do not think'—said Samuel Whiskers, pausing to take a look at Tom Kitten—'I do *not* think it will be a good pudding. It smells sooty.'

Anna Maria was about to argue the point, when all at once there began to be other sounds up above—the rasping noise of a saw; and the noise of a little dog, scratching and yelping!

The rats dropped the rolling-pin, and listened attentively.

'We are discovered and interrupted, Anna Maria; let us collect our property—and other people's,—and depart at once.'

'I fear that we shall be obliged to leave this pudding.'

'But I am persuaded that the knots would have proved indigestible, whatever you may urge to the contrary.'

'Come away at once and help me to tie up some mutton bones in a counterpane,' said Anna Maria. 'I have got half a smoked ham hidden in the chimney.'

So it happened that by the time
John Joiner had got the plank up—
there was nobody under the floor
except the rolling-pin and Tom Kitten
in a very dirty dumpling!

But there was a strong smell of rats;
and John Joiner spent the rest of the
morning sniffing and whining, and
wagging his tail, and going round and
round with his head in the hole like a
gimlet.

Then he nailed the plank down
again and put his tools in his bag, and
came downstairs.

The cat family had quite recovered.
They invited him to stay to dinner.

The dumpling had been peeled off
Tom Kitten, and made separately into
a bag pudding, with currants in it to
hide the smuts.

They had been obliged to put Tom
Kitten into a hot bath to get the butter
off.

John Joiner smelt the pudding; but he regretted that he had not time to stay to dinner, because he had just finished making a wheel-barrow for Miss Potter, and she had ordered two hen-coops.

And when I was going to the post late in the afternoon—I looked up the lane from the corner, and I saw Mr. Samuel Whiskers and his wife on the

run, with big bundles on a little wheel-barrow, which looked very like mine.

They were just turning in at the gate to the barn of Farmer Potatoes.

Samuel Whiskers was puffing and out of breath. Anna Maria was still arguing in shrill tones.

She seemed to know her way, and she seemed to have a quantity of luggage.

I am sure *I* never gave her leave to borrow my wheel-barrow!

They went into the barn, and hauled their parcels with a bit of string to the top of the hay mow.

After that, there were no more rats for a long time at Tabitha Twitchit's.

As for Farmer Potatoes, he has been driven nearly distracted. There are rats, and rats, and rats in his barn! They eat up the chicken food, and steal the oats and bran, and make holes in the meal bags.

And they are all descended from Mr. and Mrs. Samuel Whiskers—children and grand-children and great great grand-children.

There is no end to them!

Moppet and Mittens have grown up
into very good rat-catchers.

They go out rat-catching in the
village, and they find plenty of employ-
ment. They charge so much a dozen,
and earn their living very comfortably.

They hang up the rats' tails in a row on the barn door, to show how many they have caught—dozens and dozens of them.

But Tom Kitten has always been afraid of a rat; he never durst face anything that is bigger than—

A Mouse.